If You Were Born a Kitten

BY **Marion Dane Bauer**

ILLUSTRATED BY **JoEllen McAllister Stammen**

Simon & Schuster Books for Young Readers

A NOTE FROM THE ARTIST

This book was so refreshing for me because I tried something new. For
the first time in illustrating I used dry pastel on dark gray pastel paper.
I worked big—much larger than the size of the printed pieces—and this
allowed me to get the detail I needed and the color I've been looking for.
I hope you enjoy looking as much as I enjoyed creating.

SIMON & SCHUSTER BOOKS FOR YOUNG READERS
An imprint of Simon & Schuster Children's Publishing Division
1230 Avenue of the Americas, New York, New York 10020
Copyright © 1997 by Marion Dane Bauer
Illustrations copyright © 1997 by JoEllen McAllister Stammen
SIMON & SCHUSTER BOOKS FOR YOUNG READERS is a trademark of Simon & Schuster.
Book design by Paul Zakris
The text for this book is set in 26-point Berkeley Oldstyle Medium
Printed and bound in the United States of America
First Edition
10 9 8 7 6 5 4 3 2
Library of Congress Cataloging-in-Publication Data
Bauer, Marion Dane.
If you were born a kitten / by Marion Dane Bauer ;
pictures by JoEllen McAllister Stammen. — 1st ed.
p.   cm.
Summary: Simply describes how various baby animals come into
the world and what happens when a human baby is born.
ISBN 0-689-80111-4
1. Animals—Infancy—Juvenile literature. [1. Animals—Infancy. 2. Birth.]
I. McAllister, JoEllen Stammen.
QL763.B37 1997
591.3'9—dc20 96-7408

In celebration of the birth of Connor Dane Bauer
November 2, 1994

—M. D. B.

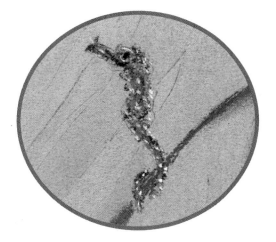

To the giver of the gift of life

—J. M. S.

If you were born a kitten,
you'd slip into the world in a
silvery sac, and your mother
would lick, lick, lick you free.

If you were a baby seahorse, you'd pop out of your father's pouch and swim away with hundreds of sisters and brothers.

If you were a chick, you'd peck and nap, peck and nap. You'd peep inside of your shell. Then you'd kick with your big feet and burst out. Hello world!

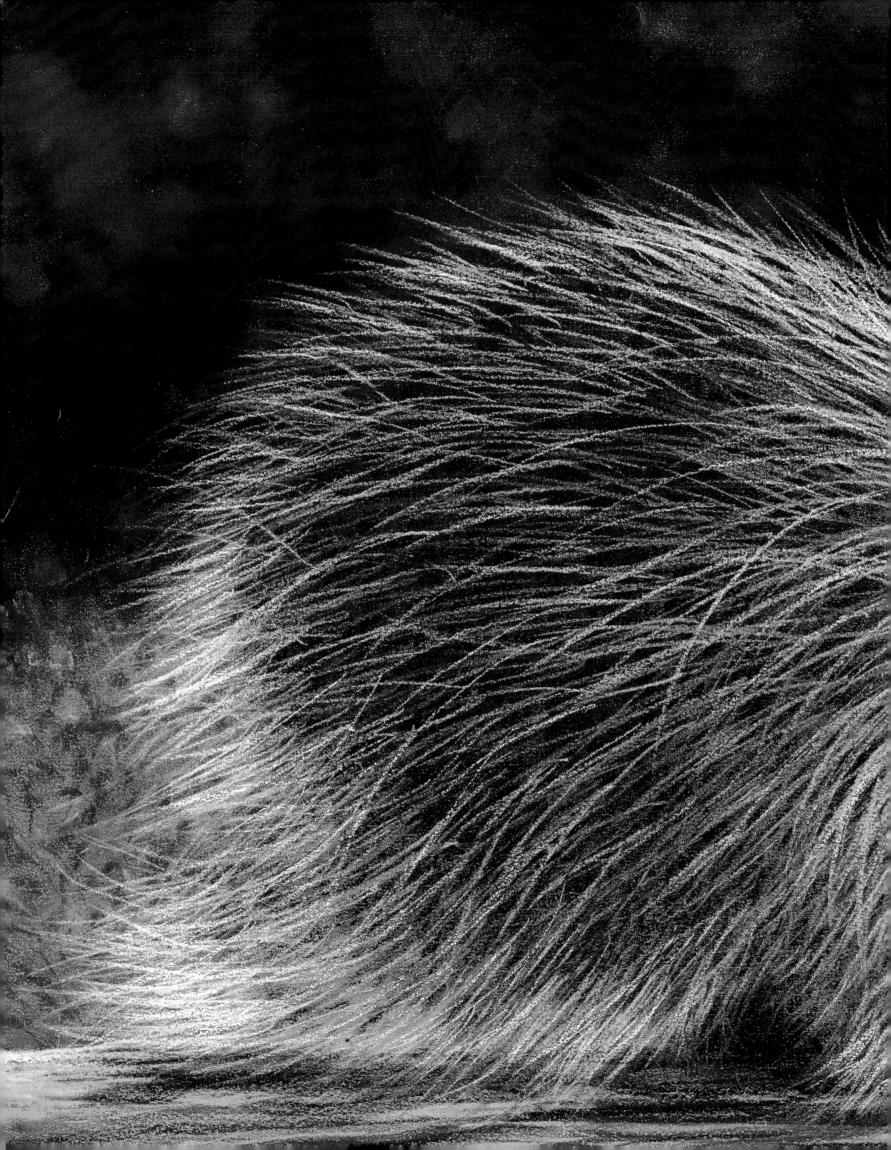

If you were a soft, new porcupette, you'd say, "Uh-uh-uh." But your prickly porcupine mother would say nothing at all.

If you were born a whale, you'd squeeze out slowly, tail first. Then your mother would nudge you up, up for your first sip of air.

If you were a
newborn opossum, you'd
fit into a teaspoon . . . with
lots of brothers and sisters.
Your mother would lick you a path
so you could climb to her pouch.

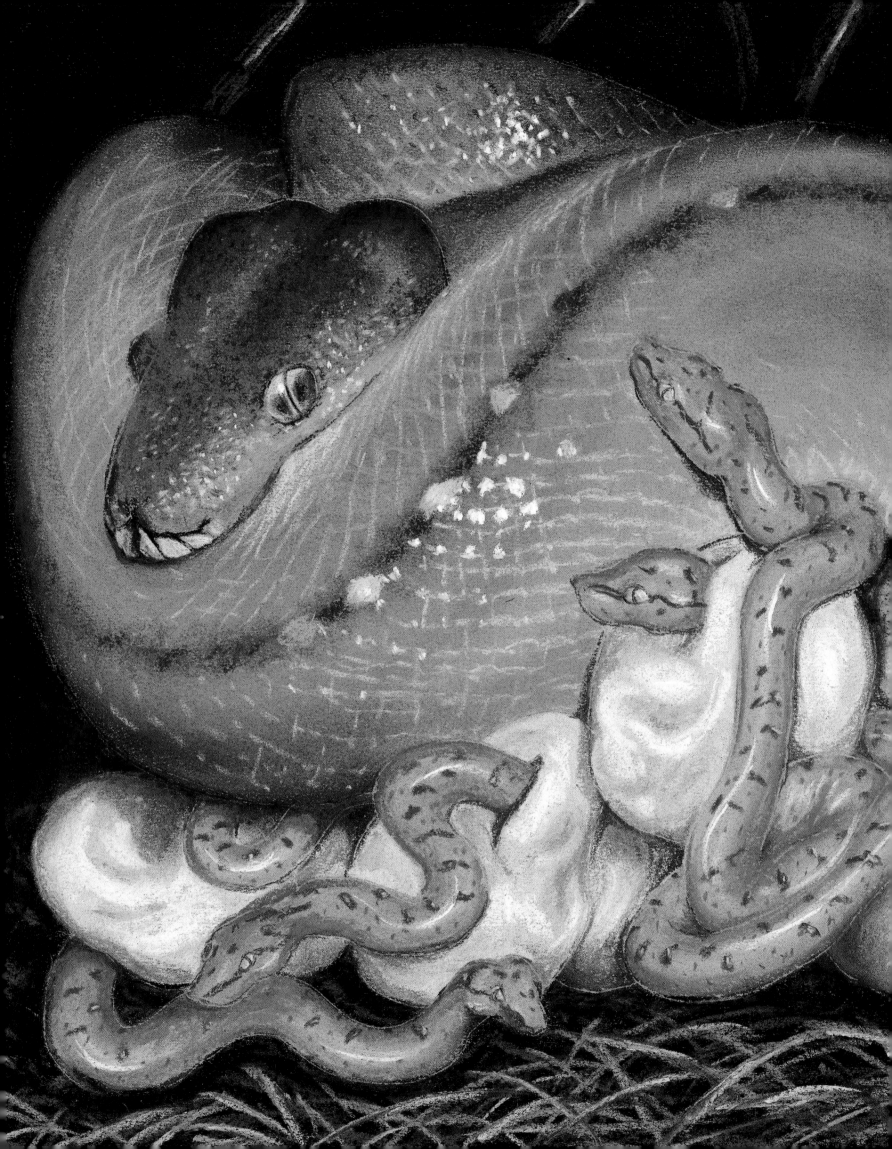

If you were a baby snake, you'd have a tooth on your snout to slash your leathery egg. "Sssss," you would say as you slithered away. "Sssss."

If you were a bear cub, you'd
come naked into a wintry den.
But your sleeping mother would
be furry and warm.

If you were a baby deer mouse, your skin would be wrinkled and pink . . . and so thin that the milk in your tummy would show through.

If you were a brand new elephant, you'd wear a halo of long, brown hair. Sometimes you might suck your trunk like a thumb.

If you were a tadpole,
you wouldn't look a bit
like your mom and dad . . .
not yet, anyway.

Of course, you're not a tadpole. You're not a snake or a porcupette or a whale. You're not a hairy elephant baby or a seahorse, popping out of your father's pouch. And yet you were born, too.

You rode curled beneath your mother's heart, growing and growing. You floated in a salty sea, waiting and waiting. Waiting for us who were waiting for you. "We're ready," we said. And you were ready, too. So you squeezed out, wailing.

Naked as a bear cub.

Soft as a porcupette.

Wrinkled as a deer mouse.

Free as a kitten.

You.